KU-471-130

OXFORD
UNIVERSITY PRESS

Great Clarendon Street, Oxford OX2 6DP

Oxford University Press is a department of the University of Oxford. It furthers the University's objective of excellence in research, scholarship, and education by publishing worldwide in

Oxford New York Auckland Cape Town Dar es Salaam Hong Kong Karachi Kuala Lumpur
Madrid Melbourne Mexico City Nairobi New Delhi Shanghai Taipei Toronto

With offices in
Argentina Austria Brazil Chile Czech Republic France Greece Guatemala Hungary Italy Japan
Poland Portugal Singapore South Korea Switzerland Thailand Turkey Ukraine Vietnam

Oxford is a registered trade mark of Oxford University Press in the UK and in certain other countries

Text and illustrations copyright © Joanne Partis 2006

The moral rights of the author have been asserted

Database right Oxford University Press (maker)

First published 2006

All rights reserved.

You must not circulate this book in any other binding or cover
and you must impose this same condition on any acquirer

British Library Cataloguing in Publication Data available

ISBN-13: 978-0-19-279176-4 (Hardback)
ISBN-10: 0-19-279176-1 (Hardback)
ISBN-13: 978-0-19-279177-1 (Paperback)
ISBN-10: 0-19-279177-X (Paperback)

10 9 8 7 6 5 4 3 2 1

Printed in Singapore by

For Chloe Tzina

LIBRARY SERVICES FOR SCHOOLS	
03289410	
Bertrams	16.09.07
	£5.99

Cowboy Ted
and the Scary Night

Joanne Partis

OXFORD
UNIVERSITY PRESS

Cowboy Ted and his friends
had been busy all afternoon.
They were making dens.

'Beautiful!' gasped Cowboy Ted, as Pretty Kitty painted pink flowers on her box.

'Amazing!' said Cowboy Ted, as Hector tapped his hammer.

'Whoops!' giggled Cowboy Ted, as Spike's den began to wobble.

Cowboy Ted was very proud of his tent. Secretly, he thought it was the best den of them all.

'It's getting late,' said Pretty Kitty.
'We'd better go back to the toy box.'
'Oh!' grumbled Cowboy Ted.
'Can't we play a bit longer?'

'But it will be dark soon,' said Pretty Kitty,
'and you know you get scared of the dark.'

'Me? Scared of the dark?' said Cowboy Ted.
'I don't think so! In fact, I have decided
to sleep in my tent tonight.'

'Oh well, if you're sure,' said Pretty Kitty as she
followed Hector and Spike back to the toy box.

But, all alone in his dark tent,
Cowboy Ted did not feel quite so brave.

All alone, he wished that he was snuggled up in the toy box with his friends. Suddenly, Cowboy Ted heard a loud ...

CRASH!

But it was only Spike!
'I got up to look for my
scarf,' whispered Spike.
'I can't find my way back
to the toy box in the dark.
Can I stay here with you?'

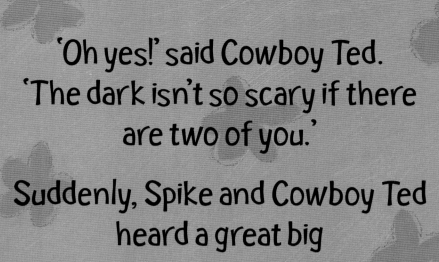

'Oh yes!' said Cowboy Ted.
'The dark isn't so scary if there
are two of you.'

Suddenly, Spike and Cowboy Ted
heard a great big

BANG!

But it was only Hector! 'I heard something go crash,' said Hector.

'I came out to check that my den was still standing but I couldn't see where I was going in the dark and I dropped my tool box.'

'Stay here with us,' said Cowboy Ted. 'Crashes and bangs are never so scary if there are three of you.'

Hector, Spike and Cowboy Ted
huddled together inside the tent.
There weren't any crashes. There weren't
any bangs. But then a silent, scary shadow
moved slowly across the wall.

'Aaaarrrrgggghhhh!'
they screamed.
'Help!'
'It's a monster!'
gulped Cowboy Ted.

'Where's a monster?'
asked Pretty Kitty calmly,
as Cowboy Ted heaved a big sigh
of relief. 'I woke up and you had
all gone,' said Pretty Kitty.
'And I was scared by myself.
Can I come in?'

'And what about the scary things out there?'
stammered Cowboy Ted.

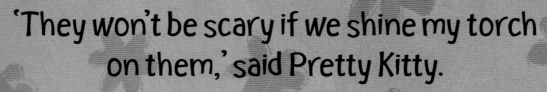

'They won't be scary if we shine my torch on them,' said Pretty Kitty.

'Look! It's just our robot,'
laughed Pretty Kitty.

'Why don't you all stay with me?' yawned Cowboy Ted.
'Sleeping in a tent is much more fun
if there are four of you.

We can put the torch outside the tent and pretend it's our campfire, just like real cowboys!'

And, one
by one,
they all
fell asleep.

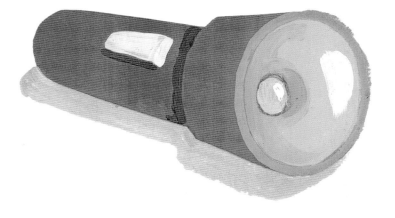